EVERY HOME NEEDS AN ELEPHANT

EVERY HOME NEEDS AN ELEPHANT

JANE HEINRICHS

ORCA BOOK PUBLISHERS

Text and illustrations copyright © Jane Heinrichs 2021

Published in Canada and the United States in 2021
by Orca Book Publishers.
orcabook.com

Library and Archives Canada Cataloguing in Publication
Title: Every home needs an elephant / Jane Heinrichs.
Names: Heinrichs, Jane, 1982- author, illustrator.
Identifiers: Canadiana (print) 2020033090X | Canadiana (ebook) 20200330918 |
ISBN 9781459824300 (softcover) | ISBN 9781459824317 (PDF) | ISBN 9781459824324 (EPUB)
Subjects: LCGFT: Graphic novels.
Classification: LCC PN6733.H45 E94 2021 | DDC j741.5/971—DC23

Library of Congress Control Number: 2020944956

Summary: In this illustrated chapter book, a lonely young girl convinces her
parents to let her adopt an elephant.

Orca Book Publishers is committed to reducing the consumption of
nonrenewable resources in the making of our books. We make every
effort to use materials that support a sustainable future.

Orca Book Publishers gratefully acknowledges the support for its publishing
programs provided by the following agencies: the Government of Canada,
the Canada Council for the Arts and the Province of British Columbia
through the BC Arts Council and the Book Publishing Tax Credit.

The artwork was created with Japanese brush pens
on Italian watercolor paper, and finished with a little bit
of photoshop magic.

Cover and interior artwork by Jane Heinrichs
Design by Jane Heinrichs and Rachel Page
Edited by Liz Kemp

Printed and bound in China.

24 23 22 21 • 1 2 3 4

APR 2 8 2021

To those who have big ideas
and even bigger hearts.

Especially Mark,
Mary, Marilyn, and the
whole team at Orca.

And to **you.**

Never forget how
extraordinary you are.

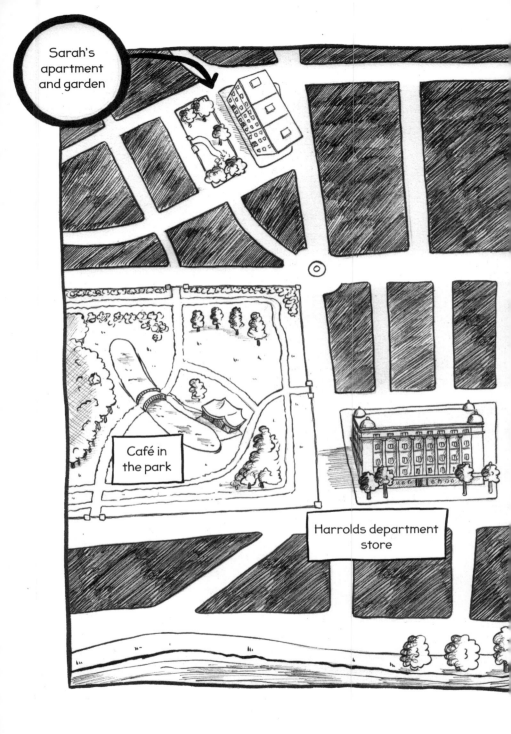

Sarah's apartment and garden

Café in the park

Harrolds department store

Small
park

Royal Bank of
Rupertsland

N

5:00 am

6:00 am

6:30 am

I sat on my thinking swing, which hung high above the stairs in our apartment, and stared out the window. I pushed my foot against the wall and swung back and forth. The hot breeze coming in ruffled the pages of my notebook.

I tapped my pencil against the blank page.

How much longer will summer holidays last?

I counted on my fingers. There were three weeks before school started again.

Three weeks was 21 days. I scribbled a few sums in my notebook. That was 504 hours. Or 30,240 minutes. Or over a million seconds.

That was a lot of time to be lonely and bored.

I was writing lists. That's what I did best. That and solving problems. The pages of my notebook were dog-eared from my fingers flipping back and forth from one list to another. From the best way to eat potatoes (never baked...yech!) to the worst smells I could think of (the storm drains on the city streets after a heavy rain).

What sort of list should I make today? I wondered. I twirled the pencil through my hair.

It was early in the morning, but it was already as hot as midday. It hadn't rained for weeks, and the roses were withering in the garden.

I smoothed my hand across my notebook and started a list of ways to keep cool.

Through the open window I heard buses rumbling down the street. I imagined where everyone might be going—to the zoo to see

the okapi or the museum to see the dinosaurs or the river to feed the ducks.

Suddenly my thoughts were interrupted by the sound of shouting and stamping. It sounded like someone was tap dancing while hollering at the top of their lungs.

I swung up to the window and peered outside. Our apartment was on the top floor of our building, and I could see the whole neighborhood spread out below me like a quilt made of brick, pavement and sun-dried grass. In the middle, surrounded by all the tall apartments, was a small green garden square that everyone living in the surrounding buildings shared.

I saw Anther, the gardener, running around and shouting.

"That blasted garden hose has sprung a leak again!" Anther hollered.

The hose flapped back and forth like an angry snake, and Anther didn't seem to be able to charm it.

Most things don't like being shouted at, even garden hoses, I thought.

"Aaahchooo!" Anther sneezed violently and tripped on the hose, which had wrapped around his ankles. He rolled under a bush and out of sight.

I closed the window, jumped off the swing and glided through the air before landing in the hallway with a thud.

I picked up the newspaper that was scattered on the stairs and noticed a colorful advertisement splashed across one of the pages. *Alone? Bored? A pet is the answer! All our fabulous pets are half price! Don't walk, run, to Harrolds department store to get yours today!*

It's too hot to run, I thought.

But a pet was the perfect solution. Maybe I couldn't buy a friend, but I could buy a pet. I could walk in the park with a pet. I could play catch with a pet. I could tell my secrets to a pet.

"Mom!" I called up the stairs. "I need a pet."

"Add it to the shopping list." Mom's voice sounded muffled behind her bedroom door.

I wasn't sure if she had heard me clearly, because she was acting like I had asked for a piece of cheese or an extra loaf of bread. Mom wasn't usually that calm when I suggested new ideas. In fact, Mom hated new ideas. The last time I'd suggested something new to her, she had sent me to my room. Mom never seemed happy with my ideas. Sometimes they *were* unusual, but not so silly that she needed to get so upset by them. The thing is, I never knew whether she would be proud of my creativity or angry that I was bothering her. So I kept trying.

I opened my mouth to mention the idea of

a pet again, but at that moment all 179 alarm clocks in the apartment started chiming.

"Breakfast!" Mom called. She raced down the stairs, scooped the newspaper off the floor and punched the button on the coffee machine. "It's 7:00 a.m.!"

I blew on my hot porridge and swirled the milk and cinnamon into spirals with my spoon.

Mom sipped her coffee and scanned the crumpled pages of the newspaper.

The doorbell chimed.

Ping! Pong!

"Hello?" Mom said into the intercom.

"It's Anther, the gardener."

"Come up," she said.

Anther came up and peeked around the doorframe.

My mom tapped her toes. "I have to leave in three minutes."

"Ahchoo!" Anther wiped his nose with a handkerchief the size of a tablecloth. "I'm sorry to bother you. I know you're busy. But...you *are* the chairperson of Pemberley Square Gardens, home of 2,000 roses, you know."

"I ordered those rosebushes from China exactly twenty-seven months ago," Mom said.

"I made a list of all their names and colors," I added and flipped through my notebook to find the page.

Anther nodded.

Mom smiled too. I knew she was proud of my lists.

"One request." He pointed a gnarled finger at the ceiling. "What with my sore leg and hayfever, I just can't cope with all the watering. Could you please hire an assistant? I need help."

"Later, Anther. I have to leave in one minute. We'll talk when I return at 5:00 p.m."

Anther sniffled.

The alarm clock by the door buzzed like a bee.

"Time to go," Mom said as she dashed down the stairs.

Anther limped after her.

Dad disappeared into his studio, which was filled with tiny gears and screwdrivers. He was working on a new clock for the train station.

All was quiet except for a low, rhythmic *thud, thud, thud* from somewhere below and the steady whirring of Dad sharpening pencils.

Dad! Mom said we could buy a pet!

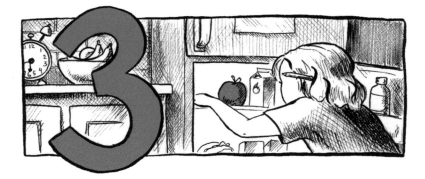

"A pet? Yes, fine…fine," Dad mumbled.

"We can get one at Harrolds. They're having a sale." I held out the advertisement, but Dad didn't look up from his drawings.

"Hmm? Oh yes, we need to get the groceries. Can you make a list? I think we're out of orange juice," Dad said.

I opened the fridge door and scanned the contents. I shook the empty milk carton and peeked into the veggie drawer, sniffing at the wilting lettuce leaves.

I flipped to a new page in my notebook and wrote, *We need everything, plus a pet.*

Brrrriiiing! The kitchen clock buzzed loudly.

"Oh, shut that thing off, will you?" Dad called from underneath his pile of sketchbooks.

Mom liked us to arrive at Harrolds department store at 9:00 a.m. sharp every Tuesday. She set an alarm on the kitchen clock for 8:35 so we wouldn't forget to leave on time. Then, because she knew we were always late, she set an alarm for 8:40 on the hallway clock to make sure we remembered to take the reusable shopping bags.

"Do you want to try some pickled eggs garnished with lawn clippings?" I asked my dad.

"You go first," he said as he examined the crackers topped with organic compost and sprouts.

The best part about shopping at Harrolds was trying all the free food samples. I always made a list of my favorite flavors.

Harrolds was a huge department store sprawling over five floors. The food hall was on the ground floor. Clothes were on the second floor. Essential things were on the third floor. Nonessential things on the fourth. And completely superfluous things were on the fifth floor. Hardly anyone ever went there but me. I loved counting the wizzygigs and drawing the thingamajigs in my notebook.

But this time, I decided that finding a pet was more important than drawing thingamajigs.

I tapped a nearby clerk on the shoulder and showed him the advertisement.

"Excuse me, sir? Can you tell me where this pet sale is? Do you have any puppies?"

"Oh, it's an *unusual* pet sale. They're all rescue animals who need good homes," the clerk said with a flourish of his hand. "The animals are lined up beside the tinned soup, but there aren't any puppies."

I took my dad's hand and led him across the store.

He balanced a tin of Peruvian sausage stew on top of the pile of groceries in his basket. "I should invent a self-collecting, turbo-jet-fueled shopping basket that does all the reaching and picking automatically."

I smiled and nodded and turned to examine the row of pets.

"Hmm?" Dad said as he squinted at the ingredients list on a tin of lentil-and-lotus-flower soup. "Oh sure, fine. Yes. Are there any preservatives in this?"

"None whatsoever. Would you like an elephant from Africa or Asia, sir?" the clerk asked.

"Which is cheaper?" Dad asked.

"They're both half price. Final sale. No returns."

"Which is bigger? I want to get my money's worth," Dad said.

"Oh, the elephant from Zimbazini, in Africa, will definitely grow the biggest." The clerk waved his arms expansively. "But they're smallish now."

"I'll take one," Dad said.

"What's his name?" I asked.

The clerk squinted at the tag around the elephant's neck. "Mr. Smith."

Dad's sundial wristwatch buzzed. "Time to pay up and head home."

"Excellent. Excellent," the clerk purred.

Every home needs an elephant! You won't regret it.

"These bags are really heavy," Mr. Smith heard Sarah complain.

"We bought a lot of tinned soup," the girl's father grunted.

"And an elephant," Sarah said.

Mr. Smith hadn't been so happy since before he was stolen from the shores of the Nambezi River. He had felt a brief surge of joy when Harrolds Department store had saved him from the poachers. But then, after the rescue, it had been exhausting to stand under bright lights waiting for someone to take him home. Now he was wandering through the park with a new family. He felt the grass under his feet—it reminded him of the grasses he had walked on in the savanna.

He nudged Sarah softly on her shoulder. He wanted to help, so he reached for the heaviest shopping bag with his trunk.

"Mr. Smith wants to carry them," Sarah said.

His heart somersaulted in his chest. She seemed to understand him, even though he hadn't said anything at all.

He curled his trunk around one bag and wrapped his tail around the other.

Sarah gave him a thumbs-up.

Mr. Smith waved his sail-like ears.

When they reached the pond, the girl and her father stopped to throw a few morsels of bread to the ducks.

Mr. Smith looked longingly at the water and and thought of the big river at home and the huge lily pads that floated in the strong currents. Their stems had reached down like anchors that clung to the riverbed to keep them from being swept away.

He had been swept away.

Far from his home and the river and wide horizons.

Some things were familiar though. The sky. The clouds. The sun. They looked the same.

Mr. Smith was sure Sarah and her dad hadn't been able to understand the bird. Not very many people could talk to animals. But that didn't matter—there were many other ways to communicate.

He picked up the bags and tickled Sarah's cheek with his tail.

He felt happy. He had a friend.

His stomach rumbled. It was a deep, loud noise because his stomach was very big and very empty.

Rummmble!

I'm going to add this to my list of reasons why buying an elephant was an excellent idea, I thought. *He's great at carrying groceries.*

I skipped down the path and shook my head in the breeze so that my hair waved in the air like a flag.

Mr. Smith wasn't just a pet. He was going to be a friend. My only friend.

At that moment the pigeon landed on the pavement at my feet.

"That was fast," I said.

The pigeon walked in circles and cooed impatiently.

I unwrapped the curled piece of paper from its leg.

Mom had underlined the word *odd* with a very thick black line. Odd was not normal. Odd was exactly what Mom tried to avoid every day. It was why she only wore gray suits to work, and why she always made the same food for dinner (meat, a carb and two veggies, never any spices) and why every day was exactly the same, even on the weekends. Mom did not like odd.

When we got home I looked at the front door.

Then I looked at Mr. Smith's large backside.

"He's not going to fit," I said.

I edged into the shade under the rose trellis and wiped my forehead. My T-shirt stuck to my back. I grabbed the damp fabric and flapped it back and forth, making a tiny breeze that cooled my skin.

Mr. Smith placed the grocery bags on the path in front of our building. He picked a rose and twirled it with the end of his trunk.

"Hmm?" Dad asked as he scraped something that smelled suspiciously like elephant poo off his shoe.

"Our elephant. I think he's too big to fit through the door."

"But he's not supposed to be full grown."

Mr. Smith buried his trunk in the jasmine.

"What's that racket?" a man's voice shouted from the ground-floor window.

"Nothing!" I yelled back.

Our downstairs neighbor, Major General N. Parker, stuck his head out his window. He didn't like noise of any sort. Loud noises. Quiet noises. Nice noises. Irritating noises. They were all the same to him. He wore earmuffs to block out the world, even on scorching summer days when it was much too hot for them.

"We're trying to figure out how to get through the front door with our shopping," I said.

"And you're disturbing our peaceful neighborhood," shouted the major general. For a man who loved silence, his voice was as loud as a foghorn in the Bering Sea.

"We'll be out of your way soon," I said hopefully.

Just then a face peered around the corner.

"Do you need any help?" she asked.

"Oh. Are you new?"

"We moved into our apartment two weeks ago. We're neighbors." Peter bounced her soccer ball down the porch stairs, and the ruffles on her dress bounced rhythmically with the ball. "Is that your elephant?"

"I've never heard of Odessia!" Major General N. Parker blared.

Peter raised an eyebrow. "It's a tiny country in Europe that everyone has forgotten."

"This is Mr. Smith." I put my hand on the elephant's warm, rough skin. "We got him this morning. He's new here as well."

Dad wheezed as he tried to shove Mr. Smith up the front steps and through the door. The doorframe splintered with a loud *crack*.

I groaned.

Mr. Smith trumpeted.

"There's got to be a better way to do it," I said. This was a problem I should be able to solve. After all, I loved problems. Solving them was my specialty. Only it was so hot...and I was so thirsty...and my brain wasn't working very well...

"We've got to get him out of the heat," I said.

Peter rummaged through our shopping bags. "How about soap?"

"Hmm?" I tried to pull Mr. Smith's left foot.

"It will make him slippery. If you rub it on his sides, he'll slide right through the door."

"That's a great idea!"

I dashed inside and zoomed up the stairs.

Once I was in our kitchen, I put three squirts of dishwashing liquid into a bucket.

"Mom wanted me to give him a bath," I said to myself. "I'm doing two things at once. She will be proud of how efficient I am."

We lathered the soap all over Mr. Smith.

I even coated the doorframe, just in case. Soap covered the roses and coated the jasmine. It sudsed down the stairs and soaked into the grass. Bubbles rose on the hot breeze and glinted like rainbows in the beating sun.

Climbing the stairs was difficult, but he wasn't
going to let it defeat him. It was the only thing that
stood between him and being part of the family.

"You can do this, Mr. Smith. All you've got to
do is take it one step at a time," Sarah said.

He looked at the long flight of stairs. *Yes!*
That was the problem. He had been going at it
backward. He'd thought he had to climb all the
stairs at once, when really he only had to climb
one step at a time.

He could manage one tiny step.

He pulled himself up.

"There are thirty-six stairs," Sarah said as she
helped him around the corner on the landing.

That didn't help, he thought with rising panic.

Be calm, he repeated to himself as his stomach lurched in his belly.

Focus on one step.

When they reached the second landing, he stopped to take a breath. He rooted with his trunk in the nearby umbrella plant, pulled off a few leaves and tossed them into his mouth. They eased the rumbling in his stomach.

Tingaling! Ting, ting, ting…ahhhh…liiiing!

"That's probably my mom calling." Sarah squeezed past him and dashed up the stairs.

Mr. Smith lumbered up the last flight of stairs and squeezed through Sarah's apartment door.

I wedged the phone between my ear and my shoulder. I could hear Mom's fingers tapping on her keyboard.

She always did more than one thing at a time. It was very efficient and also very annoying. I always felt like Mom was only half listening to me. The other part of her mind was doing complicated sums or making detailed plans.

"What are you doing?" Mom asked.

"We just got home," I said as I glanced at Mr. Smith, who was now gently stroking the fuzzy petals of the African violet on the hall table.

"You're late," Mom said. I heard her whack a stapler and then rustle some papers. "How's your new pet?"

"Fine."

"Just remember our lives are very organized, and I don't like complications."

"Nothing is complicated," I mumbled.

What could be complicated about buying an elephant? One minute you didn't have one, and the next minute you did. Simple. It's what you did with the elephant after you bought it that was complicated. But I would figure that out.

"Okay. Great. See you at five…" There was a muffled pause. "Please, could you make sure everyone's pencils are sharpened?" Then a click and the phone went dead. Mom was already giving orders to one of her employees before she had even put the phone down.

"Do you want some juice?" Mr. Smith heard Sarah ask Peter after they had unpacked the groceries.

"Yes, please," Peter said.

He watched Sarah grab a box and tip the contents into a bowl.

"Here," she said, placing the bowl in front of him. "It's all I have for now. I saw elephants eating peanuts on a documentary once. I think elephants love peanuts."

Mr. Smith stared at the small golden ovals in the bowl. He had never seen a peanut in his life, but he was willing to give it a try. He picked one up with his trunk, popped it into his mouth and chewed thoughtfully. It was crunchy, nutty and tingly. His mouth felt dry, and his throat started to tickle. He ran his tongue over his lips.

"They're salted," Sarah said. "I couldn't find plain ones."

The salt made him extremely thirsty, but he didn't know how to tell Sarah.

A small shadow darted through the door and under the table. Mr. Smith took a step back, trod on the recycling box and knocked the bowl of peanuts to the floor. *What was that?* It was something small that scurried.

Mr. Smith sneezed! Percy flew out of Peter's arms and clung to the chandelier above the table. The flower boxes on the windowsill of the open kitchen window wobbled, then tipped over, falling to the pavement below with a crash. Both glasses of juice toppled to the floor and shattered into a zillion pieces.

"Aaaahhhhhchoooo!" Mr. Smith sneezed again.

Percy shrieked, jumped off the chandelier, and disappeared behind the fridge.

"I think Mr. Smith is allergic to cats," I said.

"What's going on in there?" Dad shouted from his studio.

"Nothing!" I said. Which wasn't strictly true, but I certainly didn't want to bother him with something as insignificant as an elephant destroying our kitchen with a sneeze.

And Mom should definitely never find out. She would consider it a major complication.

I grabbed a dustpan and broom and swept all the glass shards into the pan. I stuck my head out the window and looked at the broken window boxes below. I would deal with those later.

I saw Anther trimming the roses near the front door.

The doorbell chimed, and it sounded like a chorus of cymbals heard through a very long, narrow pipe, or like chipmunks playing xylophones in the air vents.

"Act normal," Peter said. She perched on a chair, lifted an empty teacup to her lips and curled her little finger into the air.

I looked at her and raised an eyebrow. She didn't look normal at all.

The doorbell squawked again. This time it sounded like a seagull flying in gale-force winds.

"Answer the door!" Dad yelled.

"Maybe…hide the elephant?" Peter said. "We had a hard time getting the building manager to agree to having Percy live here. I'm not sure he would like an elephant."

How was I supposed to hide Mr. Smith?

I grabbed a lace tablecloth from the cupboard, threw it over Mr. Smith and balanced a vase stuffed with roses and lilacs on his back. If you squinted, he almost looked like a very tall ornamental side table.

The doorbell chirped.

I stood in front of the door and arranged a smile on my face.

"Everything is normal," I said under my breath.

We had a doorbell that sounded like a chorus of birds. An elephant disguised as a side table. A thinking swing hanging above the stairs. And a princess named Peter sitting at the dining-room table, balancing a soccer ball on her head and holding her teacup like the Queen of England.

This was all completely normal.

The roses and lilacs balanced on Mr. Smith's back smelled spicy and sweet, like nothing he had ever smelled before. He reached up with his trunk, pulled a rose from the vase and inhaled deeply.

The smell was both exotic and familiar. It reminded him of the jacaranda trees in the savanna that had colored the sky with clouds of purple flowers.

He took another deep breath. He felt like he was about to discover something very important about himself, maybe even his true calling.

He grabbed the vase off his back and started pulling the roses and lilacs out of the stagnant water. These flowers had sat unnoticed in the corner of Sarah's apartment for too long.

A rose here. A lily there. A little more height on this side. Something at the bottom to give a punch of color.

He pushed the last petal into place with his trunk.

Perfect.

I smiled so widely that my cheeks hurt, unlocked the door and opened it wide. It was Major General N. Parker, wearing his earmuffs.

He lifted one muff off his ear. "Won't you keep it down!" he bellowed. "I can hear you clearly downstairs. That means the noise is traveling through the empty apartment on the floor in between."

"It's not empty," Peter said. "I live there now."

"Doesn't make a difference. I can still hear you, even with these on."

"I'm sorry," was all I could think to say.

"What in the world?" Major General N. Parker's mouth dropped open, and his earmuffs fell to the floor.

I didn't want to look behind me. I already knew what the major general was looking at. The elephant. Or maybe the wizzygig intercom system that featured a cuckoo clock? Or the barometer that told the weather with real clouds and sunshine in a glass box? Right now thunderheads were glowering on the right-hand side, and it looked like there was going to be a storm this evening. But probably the elephant.

"It's—" I was about to explain.

The flower arrangement was like a fountain of flowers that had been frozen in time.

"Mr. Smith can arrange flowers," I whispered.

"Extraordinary," Major General N. Parker exclaimed. "Phenomenal!"

I wasn't sure what *phenomenal* meant, but if it was anything like "extraordinary," then it probably meant "not ordinary."

And that could only mean one thing.

Mom won't be pleased.

"Do you miss your home?" I asked Peter.

"Not really," she said.

"I wonder if Mr. Smith is dreaming of Africa," I said.

A gentle gust of wind ruffled the curtains.

"I think a storm is brewing," Peter said.

"I hope it rains. That will help Anther with all the watering. He was complaining about it this morning."

I watched dark clouds roil around in the barometer.

The hall clock struck five, and I heard a key in the lock.

"I'm home!" Mom called.

I watched her take three steps to the side table. She opened her briefcase and put a pile of papers into the in-box on the table. After dinner she would read through them and make lists of things she needed to do for the next day.

It was always the same, every evening.

"How was your day, Sarah? I see you have a friend over." She reached up and shook Peter's hand. "Pleased to meet you. It's so wonderful that Sarah has found someone to play with. She spends all her time reading books and scribbling silly ideas into her notebook."

"They're not silly ideas," I muttered.

"What's your name, dear?"

"Peter. Princess Peter of Odessia."

"How lovely," Mom said in a fake singsong voice as she tiptoed around Mr. Smith, who was napping on the landing. "We don't want to wake him."

She slipped into the kitchen and put the kettle on for some tea. I let out the huge sigh that had been stuck in my chest. It was all going to be okay.

Bang! Grummblebunga! Boom!

A huge clap of thunder echoed through the open window.

Mr. Smith woke, jumped five feet in the air and knocked over the flower arrangement.

Mr. Smith backed into a corner and made himself as small as he possibly could, which wasn't very small at all.

"Your elephant has destroyed several weeks of hard work," she said.

"Sorry, Mom. It was an accident," I said.

Mom's mouth opened and shut, like she was a fish gasping for air. She pointed at the vase on the floor and the crumpled flowers. "These were never supposed to be on this side table. They're supposed to be in the kitchen. Who put them there?"

"Mr. Smith did."

"Exactly," she said. "He's got to go."

Mom didn't seem to realize how extraordinary it was, phenomenal, in fact, that an elephant had moved the flowers at all, never mind arranged them into the most beautiful bouquet anyone had ever seen.

Do you have an answer?

Anther asked from the doorway.

"No, *I* don't." I obviously didn't have any answers for anything. I wasn't even sure that scribbling thoughts and equations into my notebook would solve this problem.

"I wasn't asking you. I was asking your mom. You said you'd have an answer for my problem by five o'clock. I need help watering the garden. It's ten past."

"I'm sorry, Anther. I haven't had a chance to think about your problem. We have a huge issue," Mom said.

"Can I help?" Anther asked.

"I don't think so," she said.

"I can take Mr. Smith," Peter offered. "He can stay with me tonight, and then we can return him to the wild tomorrow."

"What wild?" I asked. Nothing in the city was wild, except maybe the dark alleys.

"Oh, I wouldn't want to bother you and your father...King...?" Mom waved her hand as if trying to conjure something unbelievable out of thin air.

"King Peter of Odessia," Peter said.

"Yes, him," she said. "We can't bother him with an elephant. Can you return him to Harrolds?" she asked me. "How much did he cost?"

"It was a final sale. He was half price," Dad said quietly from his studio. "Is it five o'clock already?"

"Yes." Anther pointed at the clock. "It's now five fifteen. She was supposed to solve my problem by five."

Mom snorted as if she was having trouble breathing.

Everyone looked at her.

"That elephant needs to leave," she said.

"Excuse me, I need to leave too, Mrs. Jones," Peter said softly.

Great, I thought, now Peter thinks I come from an odd family. She's never going to want to talk to me again.

"This elephant can't stay in our apartment—it's too small. Honey?" Mom turned to my dad and paused for a second. "Do you think you can manage?"

"Manage what?"

"Make sure the elephant is gone by the time I'm back from work tomorrow. If you do that, I promise I won't complain about your automatic juice-squeezing machine that sprays orange pulp all over the kitchen."

"But...I already have too much work to do. What am I supposed to do with an elephant?"

"You're clever. Figure it out." She huffed loudly and stormed up the stairs.

I put my hand on Mr. Smith's side. I could feel the slow, steady rise and fall of his breathing. How could he be so calm in the face of disaster?

Anther? I need your help.

Mr. Smith rubbed his ear with his trunk.

Worse things had happened to him. But none of that mattered now, not compared to losing Sarah.

He remembered everything, and he could understand a lot, even the complicated workings of human emotions. He knew Sarah's mom cared for her, but her way of caring was to worry about the things that made Sarah different.

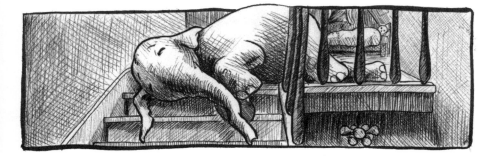

Sarah was strange in a good way. She was kind. She had a big imagination. She had interesting ideas, just like her father, and a huge capacity to show love. She also seemed to be very intelligent and stubborn, just like her mother.

Mr. Smith could see all these things, but he couldn't tell anyone his thoughts.

All he could do was arrange the flowers.

The storm raged through the night. Rain lashed the windows. Thunder rumbled from one corner of the sky to the other. I imagined that it was elephants stampeding in the sky.

The light outside my window cast shadows of tossing branches across my walls and ceiling.

I reached for my notebook, pencil and flashlight, then dove deeper under my quilt. It was hot and stuffy underneath. The rain hadn't cooled the air, but I supposed it was probably a lot hotter where Mr. Smith was from, so if he could cope, then so could I.

The flashlight clicked as I switched it on. The patchwork squares of my quilt glowed in the faint light.

I opened my notebook.

How to solve the problem of the elephant, I wrote.

I chewed the end of my pencil.

I had no ideas.

Things were pretty confusing.

First of all, there was Mr. Smith, asleep on the landing. I heard him give a whiffling snore and a grunt. He seemed so content, so unconcerned by everything that was happening around him.

Then there was Mom. I knew she loved me very much, and that was why she was so protective. Mom wanted everything to go smoothly, and that meant everything had to conform to a strict routine. It was a funny way of loving, I thought. I didn't see a lot of her because she worked so much, and when she was home we worked side by side on the daily to-do lists—washing dishes, vacuuming, tidying up…all on her schedule. Most of the time it felt like teamwork. But sometimes I wondered if all Mom cared about was her job.

The wind hurled leaves and broken branches through the air.

It was a wild storm.

Wild.

Then it came to me.

If we didn't fit into Mom's routine, then *we* would leave.

It would make life easier for everyone.

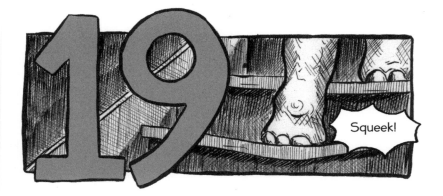

Squeek!

Mr. Smith followed Sarah as quietly as he could. The stairs buckled under his weight, and each movement made the floorboards squeak like he was stepping on a bag of mice.

He watched Sarah glance over her shoulder as if she was afraid she would wake her mom and dad up.

Mr. Smith held his breath as Sarah unlocked the fifteen deadbolts on the door. *Click!* The sound of each lock opening shot through the quiet.

He felt nervous. He needed comfort, something to quell the worry.

"Mr. Smith? Where did you go?" Sarah whispered. "How could I possibly lose a large elephant in a tiny apartment?"

All Mr. Smith could see were dark shadows and the occasional flash of lightning. He opened the garbage can in the kitchen and thrust his trunk deep into the debris. He could smell the roses among the orange peels and coffee grounds. He pulled out his trunk and showed Sarah the crumpled roses from the bouquet he had made earlier. He smoothed the petals and then arranged them behind his ear.

"Are you ready now?" she asked.

Mr. Smith nodded.

"Psst. Peter," I whispered as I knocked softly on Peter's apartment door.

Nothing but silence answered.

"She probably can't hear. The storm is too noisy," I said aloud.

I knew Mr. Smith couldn't answer, but I had the feeling he could understand. It felt comforting to talk to him. It was a bit like writing in my notebook.

"We'll go into the garden and throw pebbles at her window."

But the problem with living in the center of the city was that it was impossible to find pebbles anywhere. There was dirt, which proved too powdery to throw. There were twigs and sticks from the bushes. Or there was litter.

I scrounged through the deep puddles and found several wet, muddy bottle caps.

I lobbed one as high as I could, but it got caught on a gust of wind and flew onto the neighbor's steps. I wasn't even sure which was Peter's bedroom window. I hoped that if I managed to hit any window at all, I would be lucky enough to get the right one.

I chucked another bottle cap.

This time it hit Major General N. Parker's window. I held my breath and felt grateful that he wore those earmuffs.

"What are we going to do?" I asked Mr. Smith. "I can't throw anything in this wind."

Mr. Smith walked to a nearby bush and broke off a long stick. He reached up with his trunk and rapped the stick against the window.

But still no movement in Peter's apartment.

"I guess we'll have to run away on our own," I said.

Then I heard a faint whisper.

Peter glanced into the darkness of the apartment behind her.

"Never mind," I said. "You don't have to come."

I knew it was too much to ask. Peter was a princess. She probably had princess duties she couldn't leave behind. Besides, I was far too strange to be her friend. That was fine. Mr. Smith and I would be extraordinary—phenomenal, in fact—together in the wilds of the city's urban jungle.

That was it. We were going it alone.

I took Mr. Smith's trunk in my hand and opened the gate.

Wait!

Peter came bouncing down the front steps, dragging a heavy backpack and balancing her soccer ball on her head.

"So where are we going?" she asked.

I looked down the street. It was dimly lit by streetlights. Wind lashed the trees, and debris skittered across the pavement.

"It's lovely out, isn't it?" she said.

"Let's head for the park," I said. I stepped onto the sidewalk and turned left.

The city looked different in the dark—not scary, exactly, but unfamiliar and slightly menacing. I saw all the same houses, and all the same cars parked on the street, but everything was transformed. Major General N. Parker's jeep looked like a rhinoceros ready to charge. The tree branches were like arms flailing in the storm, grasping at the world with their sharp twigs.

I knew the way to the park. I could walk there with my eyes closed. It was fifteen steps to the corner. Then a right turn. Then across the busy street, which was quiet now in the dead of night. Then thirty steps. Then across another busy street. Then through the park gate.

Peter tiptoed in front of Mr. Smith. She readjusted her backpack on her shoulders and stood tall, staring into the dark night.

"Aahhh!" Mr. Smith raised his trunk. "Aaaaahhhchooooo!"

The force of his sneeze knocked Peter over. She scrambled to her feet. Her backpack jiggled and jumped on her back.

"What do you have in there?" I asked.

"Percy," she said. "I couldn't leave him behind."

Mr. Smith sneezed again, and his eyes started watering.

They noticed us. "What have you got there?" a teenage boy shouted. He swaggered forward, one hand deep in his pocket. His head was hunched into his shoulders and deeply hidden by his hoodie.

"What have I got where?" I asked.

"That there behind you. Is that an elephant? Maybe *I* need an elephant."

"I'll bet we could sell him to the zoo for millions," a girl said.

As she said that, more shadows materialized from behind nearby bushes, trees and parked cars.

"You. Can't. Take. My. Elephant," I said very slowly and clearly. I made my voice sound as stern and authoritative as I could. I copied the tone Mom used when she was frustrated.

Be calm, I told myself.

The teenagers were like predators stalking their prey in the jungle.

I was wrong. The city *was* wild.

It was very dark, and it smelled like wet leaves and earthworms.

I have to do something!

I shouted.

Mr. Smith swerved to the right and down a side street. I held on to his ears so tightly that my knuckles glowed white in the darkness. I had assumed Mr. Smith would understand basic directions, and it seemed he did. Just another reason why having an elephant as a pet was a wonderful idea—they were so clever.

Mr. Smith skidded at the corner and took a sharp left turn. Past a church. Past a synagogue. Past a fancy hotel. Past sleepy little cottages with tangled wisteria growing up their walls.

I could hear the teenagers' sneakers pounding on the pavement. I could hear the wind wailing through the streets. The sounds were deafening in the dark city. It was like each of my senses had been magnified. The streetlights were ten times brighter. The dark was ten times darker. The noises were ten times louder. And the smells! The dusty earthiness of Mr. Smith's wrinkly skin. Peter's clothes, which smelled of fabric softener. And Percy, still wriggling in the backpack, who smelled like terrified cat. Amazing how I could smell the fear.

"Slow down," I whispered to Mr. Smith. We were approaching a busy street. At least, it was busy during the day.

"That was close!" I said. Lights flicked on in the houses. Sleepy people peered out of their windows.

They'll think they were having strange dreams after eating too much cheese before bed, I thought.

We had to go into hiding before it was too late.

"Into the park!" I shouted.

The gates were straight ahead of us.

"They're shut," Peter whispered into my ear. "How will we get in?"

I had forgotten that the park gates were locked at sundown and only reopened again at dawn.

I looked at my watch. Dawn was still four hours away. That was 240 minutes, or over 14,000 seconds, and at least 30,000 terrified heartbeats away.

"We've got them now!" the teenagers shouted.

"That ruddy elephant!" the taxi driver who had almost hit us yelled.

Part of me wanted to laugh. That taxi driver would never have thought, when he was drinking his cup of coffee before his shift, that he would be staring at an elephant in the middle of the night.

That was another reason having an elephant was great—it was totally unexpected.

"What are we going to do?" Peter asked.

I was out of ideas. Which was also very unusual. Normally I had several spare ideas and plans outlined in my notebook, enough to cover any eventuality. But this was a problem I could never have predicted.

The teenagers were coming toward us from one direction, and the taxi driver was stomping toward us from another.

And the gates to the park were locked.

It was raining harder. Drops the size of marbles hit the top of my head with whacking thumps.

Mr. Smith stared at the angry group on the other side of the gate. His large, overworked heart was thudding.

Thumpa. Thump. Thumpa.

He hadn't run so fast since he was a little calf. He had forgotten how hard running was. His great lungs heaved. Pinpricks of light punctured the darkness. The ground swayed under his feet.

His knees collapsed under him, and suddenly the world went black. Blacker than the dark and stormy night.

"Mr. Smith!" He heard Sarah's voice as if from a great distance.

But he couldn't open his eyes.

"He's dead!" I shouted. "Mr. Smith is dead!"

I ran my hand down his trunk. I couldn't tell if he was breathing. The faint glow from the streetlight at the gate filtered through the wind-tossed branches, casting flecks of light into the darkness as the leaves roiled in the wind. I closed my eyes and traced the elephant's ear with my forefinger. It was both soft and bumpy at the same time. Leathery.

I took a deep breath to calm my shaking.

Peter knelt down beside me and put her hand on my shoulder.

"What now?" she asked.

I shrugged. Somewhere between being chased, causing an accident and realizing my elephant was dead, I had stopped planning. Having a plan used to be so important. It used to be the one thing I looked forward to. Planning something was more fun than actually doing it.

But planning didn't matter anymore. I was in a park with a dead elephant, a princess and an arthritic gardener carrying a huge shovel.

Never in a million years could I have planned for this.

A huge shovel!

My eyes jerked from Mr. Smith to Anther standing above him. The shovel glinted in the streetlight.

Mr. Smith awoke to blackness.

Is this what it felt like to be dead?

His head hurt.

He could hear people talking.

Was it Sarah? He hoped it was. He loved Sarah.

He knew he should feel afraid. But he didn't. So much had happened to him in the past day. Who knew what would happen next? He certainly didn't, and that was a little bit exciting.

I'm not dead, he decided. Just tired and hungry.

"No," he heard Sarah say. "I won't let you. I know he's alive. I can tell. Just give him some time."

"Okay," he heard the gardener say. "But I'll have to do it before dawn. We don't want a crowd."

"We have three and a half hours then," Sarah said.

He could feel Sarah stroking his ear.

His legs were tingling with pins and needles. He tried to move them, but they were numb. At least his mind worked.

That means I'm definitely not dead, he thought.

"It's a shame, really," he heard Anther say.

"He's not dead," Sarah and Peter said in unison.

His stomach rumbled.

"What was that noise?" Sarah asked. "Maybe he feels sick to his stomach. He was almost hit by a taxi. He could be feeling sick."

"I think he's hungry," said Peter.

"That's good news," said Sarah. "I should have brought snacks. What do elephants eat?"

"Normally grass and leaves off trees."

"Do you think he likes oak leaves? Or maple leaves?"

Mr. Smith heard Sarah get up and run around, ripping branches and leaves off nearby bushes.

"I think I might have a few granola bars in my backpack," Peter said. "Maybe he'll eat those."

Mr. Smith thought that he would eat anything right now.

Mr. Smith sneezed again. "Aaaahchooooo!"

"Even though he's alive, I'm still going to have to get rid of him somehow, you know," Anther said.

"No!" Peter and I cried in unison.

"I have a job to do. Your father asked me for help."

I ran my fingers through my hair.

"You can't," I said. "You'd be arrested for killing an animal."

Anther shrugged. "Who said I was going to kill him? I just need to get rid of him."

The sky was beginning to lighten in the east. Birds were chirping in the trees. It had stopped raining, but the leaves still glistened with droplets of water.

I sat on a tree stump and held my head in my hands. I couldn't even look at Mr. Smith, I felt so hopeless.

What could I do?

It was amazing. He'd almost died, yet he was still calm enough to smell the roses, to take care of them, in fact.

Anther whistled. "Well, blow me down with a feather. I never expected this! An elephant who loves flowers. This is extraordinary! This is phenomenal!"

"That's exactly what Major General N. Parker said when he saw Mr. Smith's flower arrangement."

Anther slapped his knee.

"He arranges flowers too!" He laughed and sneezed. And laughed and sneezed.

"Are you still going to get rid of him?" I asked.

I felt like singing a song.

The sun was rising.

The storm had passed.

And Mr. Smith was safe, at least for now.

I watched as Mr. Smith picked a few roses—red, pink and yellow—and wove them into a flower crown. Then he added some leaves and a spray of small white flowers that floated like mist between the roses.

He placed the crown on my head.

Tears rolled down my cheeks.

"That crown is more beautiful than any royal jewel," Peter said.

In that moment I couldn't have been happier.

But I knew it wouldn't last long. I was definitely still in trouble.

My stomach rumbled.

"I'm hungry. Did you say you had a granola bar?" I asked Peter.

"I have a few." Peter pulled a small box out of her backpack and counted the bars. "Four. One for each of us."

"One granola bar isn't going to be enough for Mr. Smith."

"Why don't we go to the café by the lake for breakfast?" Anther suggested. "They do nice eggs."

"Sure. We can eat something. And then decide what to do next," I said.

Mr. Smith grazed on leaves he plucked from the treetops as we walked through the park. Mist rose off the lake, and ducks paddled silently across the glassy water.

What can I do for you?

I'll have toast and eggs.

Me too, please.

Make that three. And a bowl of milk for Percy.

"Twenty!? Are you feeding an elephant?"

I knew she had meant it as a joke.

"Yes," I said.

The waitress looked behind me—her eyes went as big as dinner plates.

"You're *not* joking," she said.

I rubbed my eyes and lay my head on my arm. Why did they always make café tables and chairs so hard and uncomfortable? It didn't matter. I didn't need a bed, a blanket or a pillow. I could fall asleep right here, I was so tired.

"Have a rest," Anther said. "We'll take care of breakfast."

Maybe I'm in shock, I thought. My hands felt clammy and shaky. My vision was blurred. I couldn't think straight.

Was it shock, or was it being tired and hungry after no sleep and no food?

I looked at Mr. Smith. He was standing quietly in a corner of the café, between a potted fern and an umbrella tree. He looked confused too.

I nodded at Mr. Smith. We were in this together.

Mr. Smith nodded back.

"I don't know how to pay for breakfast," I said to Anther. I had packed an extra pair of underwear and my notebook, but I hadn't thought to bring money along.

"Don't worry," Peter said. "I have my dad's royal platinum credit card. He won't mind buying breakfast for an elephant."

She walked up to the counter and offered the metallic-colored card to the waitress.

"What about my mom and dad?" I asked. "Shouldn't I tell them where I am?"

"Send them a text. Tell them you're in the park with your elephant," Peter said as she keyed her PIN into the machine.

"My dad doesn't have a mobile phone. He only communicates by sending messenger pigeons."

Peter stared at me for a moment and then shrugged. "And your mom was worried that an elephant was weird?"

"Percy," she said to the cat on her shoulder. "Go catch us a pigeon. And be gentle."

"*Mao. Gēzi,*" Percy meowed.

"*Gēzi* is Mandarin for 'pigeon,'" Peter explained.

The cat leaped off her shoulder and scooted out the door.

I closed my eyes. I could smell the eggs frying and the bread toasting. Warm sunshine glowed through my eyelids like an amber halo.

Everything was wrong, yet everything felt right. It was like I was so tired, and so confused, that suddenly everything made sense.

I was Sarah, notebook enthusiast, owner of an elephant who loved flowers—no, best friend to an elephant and also best friend to Princess Peter of Odessia, whose cat knew Mandarin.

It was unbelievable, but it made sense. In fact, I realized it was only the unbelievable things that ever made sense.

Where would Mr. Smith feel at home? I ran through a list of places. Not the zoo, not the city…no…the only logical place was Zimbazini. No one there would compare me to what my mother thought was normal. And Mr. Smith would have a jungle full of plants and flowers to love.

Moving to Zimbazini was the answer to all life's problems.

It was obvious.

"Peter," I announced. "Mr. Smith and I are going to move to Zimbazini."

"Okay," Peter said.

The waitress delivered the eggs to the table, then set a huge serving tray of toast on the floor in front of Mr. Smith and backed away very slowly.

"I can call the airport and get our pilot to book us runway time," Peter said.

I looked at her blankly.

"We have a personal jet. But we need to tell air-traffic control that we're leaving so that we have a slot on the runway. I hope Mr. Smith will fit into the plane."

I stared at the sky. Was I ready for this?

"What time would you like to leave?" Peter asked as she looked up from her cell phone.

A flock of pigeons was flying over the lake, being chased from the shore by Percy.

"At sundown, I guess," I said. "That's around nine o'clock."

"Look, here's Percy with your pigeons," Peter said, mopping up some runny egg with a piece of toast.

The cat leaped onto the table and meowed proudly. He flicked his tail in the direction of the twenty pigeons who were bobbing and circling on the pavement outside the café.

Mr. Smith held back a sneeze as he ate another piece of toast.

"I didn't need a whole flock," I mumbled. "I only have one message."

I tore a page out of the back of my notebook and scribbled a message. *Dad*, I wrote. *Meet me at Mom's bank in an hour. I have something important to tell her.*

Peter looked over my shoulder. "What are you going to say?"

"Dunno. I'll figure it out on the way there."

"Okay," I called to the flock of pigeons. "Which one of you wants to carry the message?"

Ten pigeons rose up with flapping wings, and each one of them attempted to get through the open door at the same time.

Ahchooo!

I've heard of bald eagles. But I've never heard of bald pigeons.

The pigeon bobbed forward proudly and extended his leg. I rolled up the piece of paper and tied it on. The pigeon flew away over the treetops, careering lopsidedly with the weight of the paper.

Suddenly I wasn't tired anymore. I was excited. I was taking control. I was showing my parents that I was smart and independent and could make decisions for myself.

"How are we going to get to the bank?"

I looked at Mr. Smith. He was too big to take into the subway. He was definitely too big to fit onto a bus, and he would never fit into a taxi.

"We'll have to walk," I said.

"It's a lovely morning," Peter said. "And now that we've had a good breakfast, I feel like I could do anything."

I nodded.

I *knew* I could do anything.

Mr. Smith trumpeted. He obviously felt the same way.

"Are you coming along, Anther?"

The gardener looked up from his tea. "I don't think my old bones can handle much more excitement. I think I'll stay here and watch the birds."

"Let's go," I said.

Mr. Smith stepped from the soft grass of the park onto the hard sidewalk of the city. The cement was still hot from the day before. Puddles glistened in the gutters.

He reached for a dandelion growing between the cracks in the sidewalk It had pushed its roots through a narrow crack in the cement and reached its jagged leaves toward the sun. The fuzzy yellow flower swayed in the breeze, triumphant. If plants could be brave enough to grow in this city, he could be brave too.

Did he want to go to Zimbazini?

No, it wasn't home anymore.

But how was he going to tell Sarah? He could understand, but he couldn't talk. It was impossible to simply say, "Please don't make me go back."

Buses rumbled past. People rushed by, clutching bags and briefcases. Pigeons wheeled and looped in the sky.

He loved the golden morning light. He loved all the people rushing around as if what they were doing was the most important thing in the world. He loved the little flowers and weeds growing tenaciously in every crack in the pavement.

He loved Sarah. He loved Peter. In fact, he loved the city.

And as they walked, people started following them. They turned and followed Mr. Smith without glancing at their watches to see if they would be late for work, without wondering where they were going. They followed because seeing an elephant walking down the street with two children and a cat was so extraordinary it was not to be missed.

I climbed the steep stone steps of the bank and pushed through the heavy wooden door. The entrance hall had a tall ceiling, a marble floor that shone like a mirror and a magnificent stone staircase that circled upward to the floors above.

Employees scurried up and down the stairs, carrying papers and whispering into cell phones. They walked fast and were so preoccupied with their tasks, they didn't notice that an elephant had just arrived. They typed on tablets, they scribbled notes, yet no one crashed into anyone. They dashed back and forth, in and out, without looking up, as if they were so deep in their own problems and the route was so familiar that they didn't have to pay attention to where they were going.

I walked up to the security desk and cleared my throat.

"Yes?" The guard's voice was flat and bored.

"I would like to see my mother. Mrs. Jones."

"Certainly," the guard said, without looking up from his computer. He pressed a buzzer. "She'll be down in one minute."

I counted seconds to calm my nerves. "Sixty. Fifty-nine. Fifty-eight. Fifty-seven…"

By the time I got to "three," I could see my mom descending the staircase from the top floor. Having an office so high up meant she was very important.

She gasped when she saw me. "Sarah! Where were you? I didn't know what to do! And you've brought your…elephant."

At the word *elephant* everyone in the bank stopped talking, typing and scribbling. I could feel a hundred pairs of eyes staring at me.

Another hundred pairs of eyes peered in through the doors of the bank, as the people crowded on the sidewalk waited to see what would happen next.

I forgot what I wanted to say. My tongue felt dry and thick.

At that moment I heard a familiar voice.

"Let me through! My daughter is inside. She sent me an urgent pigeon!"

Dad stumbled up the steps, shouldering his way through the crowd at the doors.

"A pigeon again?" Mom asked. I could see her hands were shaking. I wasn't sure if it was from fear, relief or anger.

"Stop!" I shouted.

Mom stared at me with an open mouth.

I pointed at her. "You! You told Dad to get rid of Mr. Smith." Dad made a strangled sound behind me. "And then he told Anther to get rid of the elephant."

"But neither of them did it, by the looks of it," Mom said with a sigh.

"Anther saved Mr. Smith's life. And Mr. Smith saved my life." I cleared my throat again. "Actually he saved us from a bunch of scary teenagers and from almost getting run over by a taxi."

"Really?" Mom looked at Peter with disbelief. Peter nodded.

"Why can't you be more like Peter?" she asked. "Why can't you have a normal pet, like a cat?"

"In fact," I said, "Percy is not a normal cat at all. He is teaching Peter Mandarin."

"*Shi*," Percy meowed.

"That means 'yes' in Mandarin," Peter said.

"Oh, please! You've got to be kidding." Mom threw her hands into the air.

"Sometimes I don't think you even care about me!" I shouted. "All you care about is your career and what everyone else thinks of you."

Mom looked around at the hundreds of faces.

"All I want is the best for you," she said. "I want you to be successful. But all you do is wander around with your nose in your notebooks, ignoring everything I say."

I crossed my arms, took a deep breath and decided to ignore what she had just said.

"Where are you going?" Dad asked.

"To Zimbazini, where Mr. Smith is from. Since he's my best friend now, I don't want to lose him."

Mom made a choking sound.

"I want to go somewhere where I can be myself. I'm tired of trying to fit in. I think your life would be easier without me. So I'm going," I said firmly.

"If that's really what you want..." Mom said, her voice trembling.

I stared at my feet. My sneakers still had grass stuck to them from our walk through the park. This wasn't the answer I had wanted to hear. I had wanted Mom to be shocked, but I had also hoped that she would fight for me. That she would tell me how much she loved me. That everything would change.

I swallowed hard. It felt like my fried eggs and toast were stuck in my throat

"Mrs. Jones," Peter said softly. "Are you sure?"

Mom was also staring at her feet. After a long silence she said, "Of course I don't want Sarah to leave. But I don't know what to do. She seems so unhappy. And I don't know how to make it better. My version of happy and her version of happy are completely different."

"Yes, there are many kinds of happiness," Peter agreed. "And I'm not sure Sarah would be completely happy if she left either."

"What do you mean? Of course I would be! Anything would be better than here."

"You would miss your mom and dad."

Mom put her hand on my shoulder. "Sarah, my life might sometimes be easier without you, but it wouldn't be happier. Some complications bring more joy than frustration."

I stomped my foot on the floor. Grass clippings scattered all over the shiny, clean tiles. "C'mon, Mr. Smith. We're going to the airport."

Mom climbed the first few stairs very slowly, her trembling hands holding on tightly to the banister. She stopped and gently touched the petals of the roses twining up the columns. Then she bent over, nestled her nose into one of the blooms and took a deep breath.

"I think we need to consider everyone concerned," she said. "It's not just you and me, but also your father and Peter and Anther and even Mr. Smith. I know your father doesn't want you to go. I'm sure Anther doesn't either. So that leaves one opinion we don't know."

"Whose?" I asked.

"I can't believe I'm doing this," she said as she turned to Mr. Smith. "I'm about to talk to an elephant."

She cleared her throat.

"You seem to have an extraordinary understanding, for an animal. Would you be happier back where you came from?"

"Of course he would!" I shouted.

Mr. Smith pushed through the crowds of people. Cars whizzed by in one direction, and buses rumbled past in another.

Where was he going?

He wasn't exactly running, but he was going as fast as he could while trying to dodge surprised pedestrians. People stared, but that was fine. He knew he was unusual. People kept telling him he was "extraordinary!" and "phenomenal!"

Behind him he heard shouting.

"Mr. Smith!" Sarah called.

"Come back!" Peter shouted.

He listened to their voices echoing between the tall buildings. The windows glittered and shone in the hot summer sunlight, reflecting the sky.

It looked like there was the great sky overhead and then hundreds of pieces of sky pasted to the brick walls. Like squares of glitter raining down.

Mr. Smith plucked flowers from the window boxes and made tiny flower arrangements as he ran.

He thought about the look on Sarah's face when her mother said that life might be easier without her.

She hadn't meant it, of course. At least, not really.

He thought Sarah's life would be easier without him. But he couldn't tell her that.

All he could do was disappear.

I dodged.

I ducked.

I poked my head into dark doorways and narrow alleys.

Mr. Smith was nowhere to be seen.

"Wait!" I heard Peter shout from some distance behind me.

"Stop!" Dad hollered.

"We have to have a plan!" Mom added.

For a second I wondered why Mom was part of the chase. Then I tripped on someone's feet and scrambled to steady myself.

I'd thought I had a plan, but everything was upside down. Plan A hadn't worked (get an elephant as a pet), plan B had been a disaster (run away with elephant to the park), plan C had made me a laughingstock (the elephant had abandoned me).

How on earth could plan D work?

What was plan D anyway?

No…plans were useless.

I wanted to use my instincts now. I wanted to run. My arms pumped up and down, and my lungs inhaled and exhaled like huge bellows fanning a fire.

"Mr. Smith!" I shouted. "Mr. Smith! Come back!"

My heart clenched. It was hopeless. Why hadn't I asked Mr. Smith if he wanted to leave? I hadn't even considered the possibility that he wouldn't want to.

I had made assumptions.

I was exactly like my mother.

I was starting to understand. It was so easy to want the best for someone and not actually ever find out what that person really wanted.

"Sarah!" Peter called.

Peter ran up to me and rested one hand on my shoulder as she clutched her side with the other.

I shaded my eyes with my hand and squinted down the street. There were tall buildings and buses and cars and people. All the things you would expect to see in a city. But I didn't see the one thing you would never expect to see—an elephant.

"Um," Peter said. "I hate to be the voice of reason."

"Don't be then." I shrugged Peter's arm off my shoulder.

"Here we are, running down the street. But where are we running to exactly? We are running to nowhere in particular and shouting out the name of a missing elephant. And there are ten men named Mr. Smith following us, thinking we're calling for them. It doesn't make sense."

"Do you have a better idea?" I asked.

"We should try to think of somewhere Mr. Smith would go."

"Yes," Mom added as she jogged up to us. "That would be both logical and rational."

"Why do you care?" I yelled. "Earlier you wanted to get rid of him."

"If he's important to you, he's important to me too."

"Really?" I asked.

"Yes," Mom said. "I was mistaken. I need to listen to you more."

"And I should have listened to Mr. Smith," I said.

"Then we all need a few lessons in listening," Mom said.

"Where would he go?" Peter asked again.

I didn't have any answers. I felt a desperate panic clutch at my chest. I turned and cupped my hands around my mouth.

"Mr. Smith!" I screamed.

"The thing is," Peter said, "he ran away on his own. He probably doesn't want to be found. Bellowing his name will warn him you're coming, and he'll be more likely to run away again."

"Okay," I said. "You're right. Let's make a plan. We'll call it plan D."

"All plans start with a point of origin," Mom said.

"Perfect. Somewhere to start from. Anyone know where we are?" Peter asked. "I'm new here. I don't know my way around."

"I'm not entirely certain," Mom said.

"No idea," I said.

"Great," Peter said. "We have no idea where we are, and we have no idea where we're going."

Lost, I thought. That word meant so many things.

Mr. Smith looked both ways. Then he looked behind him for good measure. All clear. No traffic. No Sarah behind him.

He was following his nose. He could smell roses somewhere. He knew he would be safe anywhere roses grew.

They were beautiful but also thorny.

He squeezed into a narrow alley. The rough bricks scratched his sides. From somewhere behind him he heard the clamor of running feet. But the alley was so small, he didn't have room to turn his head to look behind him.

He emerged into a wide, sunshiny square and peered down the alley he had just left. Several small shapes were charging toward him. They didn't look like Sarah and Peter.

Whoever they were, they didn't look friendly.

He thrust his trunk into the air and searched for the scent of roses. It was almost lost in the smells of exhaust fumes, coffee grounds and ancient sandwiches rotting in the garbage can beside him.

There! He caught the heady floral fragrance.

He veered right and started to charge ahead.

All is lost.

He who hesitates is lost.

Lost for words.

Lost soul.

Make up for lost time.

Lost in thought.

I'd made a mental list of all the ways I could use the word *lost*.

But actually *being* lost was different. The phrases couldn't describe the feeling of hopelessness and fear.

And being lost without having a destination was another problem entirely. If I didn't know where I was, and I didn't know where I was going, then what was the point?

It was a lost cause.

My feet and head hurt. My eyes watered from the glaring sunshine.

I inched backward into a patch of shade.

A daisy stuck to my shoe. Its petals were trampled brown, and its leaves were wilted.

I picked it up and held it to my nose. Daisies, I discovered, didn't have much fragrance. This was something Mr. Smith would have probably known.

"Let's see," Mom said. "If that way is north, then I think that's Main Street up ahead. So we're not truly lost."

"Where to then?" Peter asked.

"I don't know," I said.

I knelt down and knotted my shoelaces. There were more daisies on the sidewalk, scattered around my feet.

"Look!" I said. "There is a trail of daisies leading all the way down the street!"

Flowers.

Of course.

Flowers!

I grabbed Peter's hand.

Follow the trail of flowers!

Mr. Smith was being chased by the group of hoodie-wearing teenagers.

He clutched the last ragged daisy in his trunk like a talisman. Everything would be okay if he still had a flower.

He scooted around a corner.

There.

There were the roses he had been seeking.

He had arrived in a quiet, leafy garden square. In the middle, nestled among the trees, was a beautiful rose arbor.

"He's gone that way!" he heard the kids shout. It wouldn't be long before they found him.

He walked onto the soft, mossy grass. He could smell the roses that climbed up the columns and twined through the arbor. Pigeons swooped in and out, dancing with the clouds above.

He was sure he would be safe there.

In one section the climbing roses made a long screen between the stone columns. He slipped behind it and sat on the cool stone floor.

No one would find him here.

He twirled the daisy in his trunk and counted the blades of grass growing between the huge flagstones on the ground.

He heard quiet footsteps.

Sarah? he wondered.

He peered through the climbing roses and saw a shadowy shape walking through the arched doorway.

Was it her?

Mr. Smith shifted his legs, and the leaves rustled.

"Over there," the boy whispered, and pointed at the roses.

A girl tiptoed across the sanctuary.

"We've got him. He's trapped. Hand me the shovel. I'll try to hit him on the head and knock him out. Then we can take him to the zoo for a reward."

"Think you're strong enough?"

Mr. Smith shuddered.

The kids were right. He was trapped.

What could he do?

He looked around frantically for an escape route, but all he saw were stone walls and thorny roses.

That's it!

Sarah was out there somewhere. He was wrong to have run away. Sarah would find him.

"What's he doing?" shouted the girl.

Mr. Smith stripped thorns off the climbing roses and laid them in a pile at his feet.

If they came too close, he had ammunition.

I picked the daisy off the sidewalk and handed it to Peter.

"This is the last one," I said.

I scanned the pavement around me. The trail of daisies had guided us through the city for three blocks.

"Are you sure?" asked Peter.

There were all sorts of ridiculous things littering the pavement—gum wrappers, half-eaten sandwich crusts, a lost smartphone, baby soothers, plastic bags and a lone shoe.

But there weren't any more flowers.

I bent down to examine the smartphone. The screen was cracked like a spider's web.

"What are you doing?" Peter asked.

"I'm simply Exploring alternate methods of communication."

Mom was marching ahead and shouting Mr. Smith's name.

"Extraordinary," I said, staring at the broken phone.

Everything was extraordinary when you looked at it long enough, even the rubbish lying on the sidewalk. Take that pencil stub lying in the gutter, I thought. It might have been used to draw masterpieces in a sketchbook. It was extraordinary.

"Well, if you two are going to stand around staring at rubbish, I suppose I should carry on with the search," Dad said. He grabbed the bunch of wilting daisies and peered at his compass.

"Can you see them?" I panted. I stumbled over a discarded bicycle helmet.

"No—oh yes. There. Between the skyscraper and the brick tower." Peter pointed to a patch of sky.

Percy clung to her shoulder and meowed. "*Pǎo!*"

"That means 'run' in Mandarin," Peter translated.

"Oh!" I gasped. "I think I could have figured that out."

"The problem with running after birds in a city," Mom said between breaths, "is that they can fly anywhere they want in a direct line.

As the crow flies, or as the pigeon flies, so to speak. But we have to stick to the streets."

Dad held his compass high above his head. "They're heading due east."

"Is that significant?" Mom asked.

"Where does that mean they're going?" I asked.

"No idea," Dad said.

Sometimes, I thought, information was just information, and not really helpful.

I caught a glimpse of the rose-carrying pigeons disappearing over a nearby rooftop and pointed. "There!"

I forced my legs to run faster. My lungs were burning. I didn't want to run anymore. But I had to. My arms pumped back and forth. The notebook in my toolbelt slapped against my thigh, and the rhythm sounded like a heartbeat.

The pigeons were overhead now. Their roses were losing petals in the hot summer wind, which rained down around them, fluttering to the pavement like confetti.

I ignored my muscles, which were screaming at me to stop running.

I turned the corner.

"GET ME THAT ELEPHANT!" I heard a boy shout. The voice was gruff and mean. I recognized it from somewhere. My mind whirred, spinning backward through all my memories. The café. The park. The escape in the night…

It was the teenagers.

My heart lurched.

"WHOOOPA!" Mr. Smith trumpeted.

I could just see him, trapped behind a rose arbor.

Fear prickled the back of my neck.

"STOP!" I shouted.

Mr. Smith broke off another rose branch and rubbed his trunk over the stalk. The sharp triangular thorns snapped off and fell into a pile at his feet. With each one that dropped, he named a worry. Nothing seemed to matter when he thought of all he had to lose now. Sarah. Friendship. Flowers. Mounds of hot buttered toast. The way the weeds grew between the paving stones, against all odds.

He had been stupid to run away. This was all his own fault.

"It's not personal," the boy snarled as he stalked closer.

Mr. Smith held himself very still. In fact, he wondered if he had stopped breathing altogether. Nowhere was safe. He didn't belong anywhere.

Sarah dashed forward and tried to grab the boy.

The boy put his foot out and Sarah stumbled, somersaulted across the cobbled floor and crashed into Peter, who fell on her backside.

"Hey! You're not helping!" Peter shouted.

"*MEOW!*" Percy flipped off her shoulder and scrambled across the courtyard in a flash. He disappeared into the climbing roses and scooted up the column until he was sitting high above the fray.

Mr. Smith felt his trunk tickling. From deep inside him a sneeze was about to erupt. He tried to hold it in.

"Hich-hee," he hiccuped.

The sneeze was still tickling. He could feel it building up from the bottom of his toes. He scrunched his eyes closed. He clamped his feet over his trunk. But he couldn't hold it in.

"AAAAAAHCHOOOOOO!"

"Duck!" Sarah's dad shouted.

The force of Mr. Smith's sneeze sent the pile of rose thorns flying everywhere.

"Ow! Ow! Ow! Ow!" the boy wailed. "I've been hit."

"Are they gone?" I asked.

"I think so," Peter said.

"*Shi*," Percy meowed.

"He says 'yes.'"

Mr. Smith edged his way out from behind the climbing roses.

I stared at him. Even though he was a largish elephant, he seemed so small, suddenly, in the vastness of the city. So alone. And lost.

"Are you okay?" I asked Mr. Smith. This was the first time I'd asked Mr. Smith a question. Why hadn't I thought of it before?

Mr. Smith shook his head slowly. Then he nodded. Then he shook it again.

"I feel exactly the same way," I said. I stepped forward with my arms outstretched.

I'd thought I had all the answers, but now I knew that wasn't true. The only way to find an answer was to start asking questions.

I looked at my mom, who was crouching on the ground, sweeping the sharp thorns off the stone paths with a broom made of leaves and twigs. Mom was always doing something useful, I thought.

My dad was examining a handful of thorns with a look of faraway inspiration on his face. He was probably inventing something.

Everything had changed. And nothing had changed.

"What are we going to do?" I asked again.

At that moment Anther came charging through the trees.

"What's going on? I was sitting at the café, having my fifth cup of coffee, when I saw pigeons flying around carrying roses. So I followed them, because I thought they were ruining one of the city's beautiful rose gardens. Then I saw a group of teenagers hotfooting it away, completely covered in thorns. I thought there must have been a grand battle, and all the roses were ruined. Nothing, *nothing*, excuses the ruining of a rose!"

Mr. Smith trumpeted in agreement and handed a thornless rose to Anther.

I think I have the answer.

"All I have ever wanted to do was make things right," Mom said. "I wanted us to be a normal, happy family."

"Is there really such a thing as a normal family?" Peter asked and then buried her head in Percy's fur.

"But Mr. Smith has taught me something very important," Mom continued. "When you ran away and I thought I had lost you, Sarah, I started to rethink everything. And when Mr. Smith ran away and I saw how much you cared about him, I realized it is our eccentricities that make us lovable."

I walked over the cobblestones to my mom. I didn't have to worry about stepping on thorns, because she had already swept them away. That somehow meant everything. Mom made things safe and orderly. That was *her* lovable eccentricity.

"Mrs. Jones?" Peter asked. "You said you had the answer?"

"Oh yes," she said as she wiped a tear off her cheek. "Anther, I have found you a gardening assistant."

"Oh?" Anther said.

"Who?" Sarah asked.

"Mr. Smith, of course," she said. "I have reviewed his talents, and it seems to me that no one could be better suited to gardening. He loves flowers almost as much as he loves Sarah. He is big and strong, so he can help you with heavy work, and he has a built-in watering hose. He'll have to live in the apartment-block garden, of course. We'll build a home for him."

"And I can visit him?" I asked.

"Every day," Mom said.

That was the end, thought Mr. Smith. But it was also just the beginning. He realized that no story really ends—it just stops in an interesting place.

He loved his new home in the garden. He could see Sarah's bedroom window from his safe space. Climbing roses rambled over his roof, and they smelled like heaven. Sarah came to visit every day with Peter.

Mr. Smith looked out the window of his cottage in the garden at the pink clouds floating above the trees. He could hear the distant rumble of traffic, intermingled with the whispering of the leaves in the breeze.

Tomorrow a rose named Summer Song would start to bloom. He couldn't wait to show Sarah.

He hummed a happy tune to himself and poured water over the lilies at his feet.

A Million Thanks

When I set out to tell the story of Sarah and her elephant, I knew it was going to be different from anything I had done before. But I never guessed that flashes of inspiration, from both me and my editors, would change the book's direction innumerable times. Every author says their book wouldn't be possible without assistance; in my case, it's true.

Chronologically, the first thank-you needs to go to a renowned children's book publisher in London. Ten years ago he rejected my manuscript for a picture book featuring Sarah and her elephant. Luckily, he was intrigued enough to chat with me about it, saying he thought the story and characters were too big for thirty-two pages. I am eternally grateful for that rejection, for I realized he was right. I went back to the drawing board, and the story grew to accommodate Mr. Smith, Sarah and their adventures.

The next thanks need to go to my family: Mark, my husband; Mary, my daughter; Marilyn, my mom; and John and Sibylle, my parents-in-law. They were endlessly patient when inspiration pulled me into my studio and I buried myself in stacks of papers and notebooks. I might have gotten lost in all the papers, but I found the story.

Mark has always supported me in my work, even when the path seemed foggy. This book is the result of that unwavering belief in the future.

My mom is my alpha reader and has read every word I have ever written, from my first stories about turtles loving puddles to stories that will hopefully still make it into your hands someday and, of course, this one. Thank you for your patience.

Monique Polak, who also read an early draft, gave me the courage to send the manuscript out into the world. Without her enthusiasm, this story might still be sitting in my hard drive.

This book wouldn't exist if it weren't for the brave, creative, amazing team at Orca Books.

Thank you to Liz Kemp for seeing the possibility in a story about a small girl and a big elephant. You are such a gifted editor.

Thank you to Rachel Page for her book-design alchemy. She managed to translate what I saw in my head and made it real on the page. Transforming this story from an idea into a book was a dream come true!

Thank you to Andrew Wooldridge and Ruth Linka for taking a chance on this quirky story. I'm honored that my book can rub shoulders with the other amazing books on the shelves in the Orca office.

Others have helped this book on its journey, providing love, support and advice. Thanks to Laura, for innumerable coffees in Bloomsbury and text-chats while we commiserated about writing, editing and deadlines, and Adrienne, my neighbor and fellow creative, for being a cheerleader when I needed it most.

Thank you to all the subscribers of my email newsletter. I shared the ups and downs of my progress with you, and your replies gave me courage.

Finally, thank *you* for reading this story. You are special just the way you are.

Jane Heinrichs is a children's book author and illustrator. She grew up in rural Manitoba but now lives in London, England, with her husband and daughter. She has illustrated many books for children. She starts her day at a clear desk with her huge sketchbook (for books) and her tiny sketchbook (for daily drawings) but usually ends up sitting on the floor, surrounded by a collection of paints, pencils and papers. She doesn't have any pets, and her house is definitely too small for an elephant. However, just like Mr. Smith, she loves to garden, and her garden is full of roses.